WITHDRAWN

For the Bump
−H.O.

For my sister
−R.R.

tiger tales
an imprint of ME Media, LLC
5 River Road, Suite 128, Wilton, CT 06897
Published in the United States 2012
Originally published in Great Britain 2011
by Scholastic Children's Books
Text copyright © 2011 Hiawyn Oram
Illustrations copyright © 2011 Rosie Reeve
CIP data is available
ISBN-13: 978-1-58925-105-2
ISBN-10: 1-58925-105-9
Printed in Singapore
TWP 0611
1 3 5 7 9 10 8 6 4 2

For more insight and activities,
visit us at www.tigertalesbooks.com

My Friend Fred

by
Hiawyn Oram

Illustrated by
Rosie Reeve

tiger tales

This is Fred.

My friend Fred.

My sister, Sarah, who has lots of friends, says,

"No, Grace, he is not yours.
He is ours. Our family dog."

I do not argue but I think, No, Sarah,
you are wrong. Fred is mine.
My friend Fred.

I know he is mine because he is always there
when I open my eyes in the morning.

He is always there when
I shut my eyes at night.

And before I shut my eyes,
he always checks for monsters
under my bed.

(If there is one thing Fred will
not have in our house, it is
monsters under my bed.)

He likes the same stories I like.
My favorites are his favorites.
And he likes the pictures just
as much as I do.

When I am playing,
he plays with me.

When I am running
like the wind,
he runs with me.

When I am lying around on a beanbag
talking to myself, he lies around too.

We lie around together.

Me and my friend Fred.

And that's not all.

When I lose things, Fred tries to find them for me.
He found Max Bear the time Max got himself
dropped in the pond.

He found the shoe with the plum on it
when I thought it was gone forever.

(My shoe with the plum on it is for this foot.
It goes with my shoe with the cherry on it,
which is for this foot. Together they are
my favorites.)

Sniff!

And he always seems to know where to

find my important backpack with my name on it.

Pant, Pant!

Sniff!

Found it!

(This backpack will be my school bag when
I go to school, which could be any day now
so it is important that I do not suddenly
find I can't remember where it is.)

Even so, even with all these reasons piled up
as high as a giant beanstalk, Sarah goes on and on.

"Grow up, Grace.
Fred is ours.

Our family dog."

One day, when a lot of her friends came over,
she got a ball and said,

"Come on, Fred
the Family Dog.
Come and play
ball with us."

And that was cheating because
she knows Fred cannot say no to a ball.
Even if a giant who ate
little dogs for lunch said,
"Come on, Fred, come and
play ball with me,"
Fred could not say no.

So I picked him up, took him to my room . . .

and shut
the door tight.

"Fred," I said,
"I think there is a scary
monster under my bed."

I got out our favorite books and said,
"Let's look at these for hours and hours
until all Sarah's friends go home."

Duck Goes Cluck

Jack and the Beanstalk

When I am BIG

Scary Fairy

The Glass Slipper

Wag's Tale

Goody the Goose

But Fred did not check for anything under the bed. And he did not want to look at books with me.

Puppy Love

A Dog is not a Cat

He pressed his nose against
the window and drooled
and scratched.

He lay by my
shut-tight door
and whimpered
and whined.

I listened from behind my books
until, in a flash, I suddenly understood
what he was trying to say.

And now I did understand.
It was as clear as could be,
and I opened my shut-tight
door and we ran outside.

"All right, Sarah," I said. "Friends don't keep their friends all to themselves all of the time. So here he is.

The Family Dog.
Our friend Fred."

"Thanks, Grace," barked Fred, already leaping for the ball.

"Thanks, Grace," said Sarah's friends.

"Thanks, Grace," said Sarah.
"This is very big of you."

And I agree it **was** big of me,
but then I can be big when I
want to be, especially because
I know
"ours"
is only a **word**
and whatever anyone says,
really
that dog will
always
mostly
be . . .

my friend Fred.

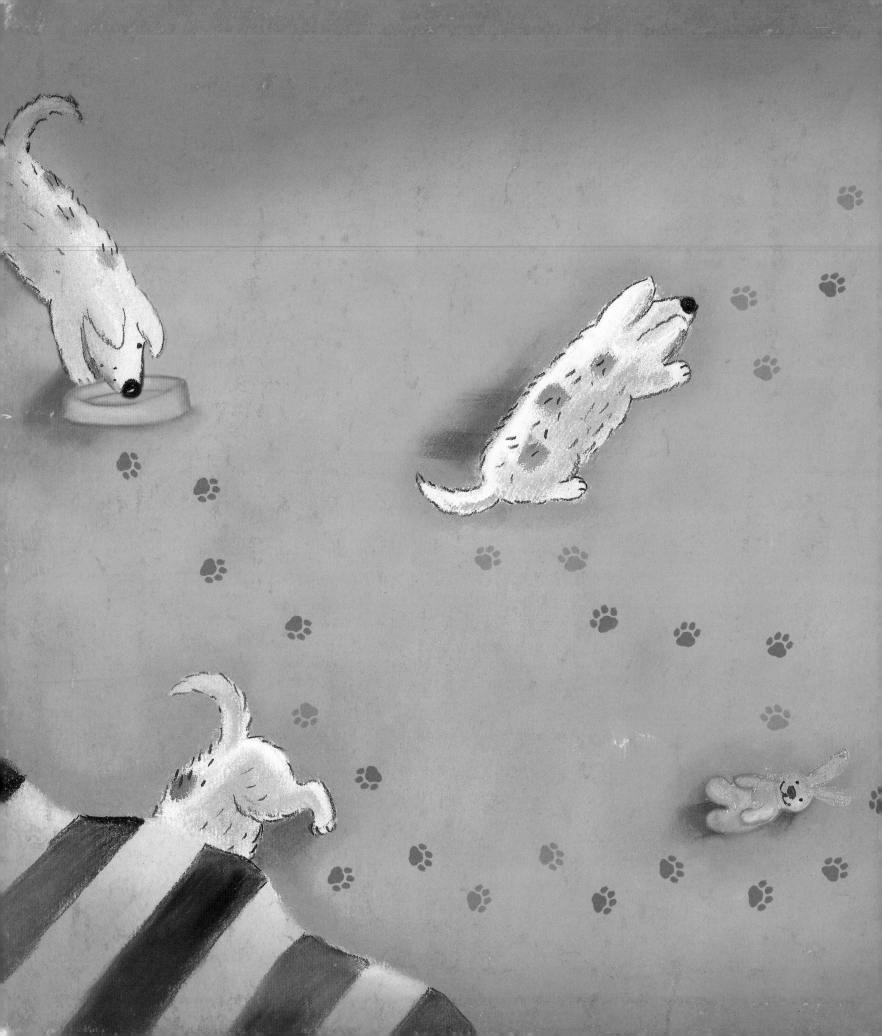